This book belongs to:

GENEVIEVE & ROSALYN

ALOHA — FROM
    BABCIA & GRANDPA —
        — 2013 —

21

Glossary

leotard (LEE-uh-tard): A leotard is a tight piece of clothing that covers the body from the shoulders to the thighs. Dancers and gymnasts wear leotards.

mini trampoline (MIN-ee tram-puh-LEEN): A mini trampoline is a piece of exercise equipment made of strong canvas attached to a frame with springs. It allows gymnasts to bounce up high.

pikes (PIKES): In a pike, the gymnast keeps the legs straight.

somersaults (SUHM-ur-sawlts): Somersaults are rolls where the head goes down on the ground and the body turns over the head. Another word for somersaults is forward rolls.

straddles (STRAD-uhlz): In a straddle, the gymnast's legs spread wide out to either side.

tucks (TUHKS): In a tuck, the gymnast's knees are bent and the legs are pulled in close to the chest.

Index

Websites

www.usa-gymnastics.org
www.fig-gymnastics.com
www.gymnasticszone.com

About The Author

Holly Karapetkova, Ph.D., loves writing books and poems for kids and adults. She teaches at Marymount University and lives in the Washington, D.C., area with her husband, her son K.J., and her two dogs, Muffy and Attila.

G is for Gecko

an alphabet adventure in Hawai'i

illustrated by **Don Robinson**

BeachHouse

Illustrations by Don Robinson
Text and design by Jane Gillespie
Library of Congress Control Number: 2013930618
ISBN-10: 1-933067-51-9
ISBN-13: 978-1-933067-51-3

First Printing, April 2013

BeachHouse Publishing, LLC
PO Box 5464
Kāneʻohe, Hawaiʻi 96744
email: info@beachhousepublishing.com
www.beachhousepublishing.com

Printed in Korea

is for the Auntie that
shoos him away.

B is for the Broom she swings with dismay.

is for the **Cat**
that chases him
about.

is for the Door
that locks Meow
out.

E is for Early on a bright Hawaiian day.

F is for the Flower he smells on his way.

G is for Gecko strolling down the street.

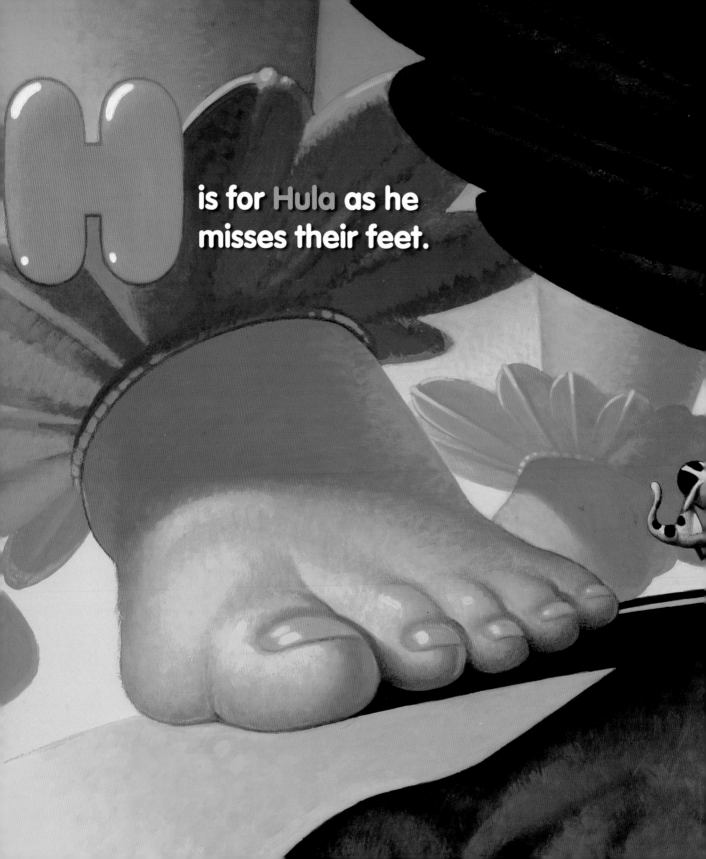

is for Hula as he misses their feet.

is for Ice making
everything wet.

is for **Jump** as far
as he can get.

is for **Kick** as he flies through the air.

is for the Lei he
lands on with care.

is for the Nēnē
waving goodbye.

is for the 'Ono food that he tries.

is for the Peacock with dozens of eyes.

is for the Quilt
spread out on
the grass.

R is for the
Runner he
allows to pass.

S is for the **Surf** slipping onto the shore.

is for the Turtle
starting to snore.

U is for **Under** the coconut tree.

is for Visit with friends by the sea.

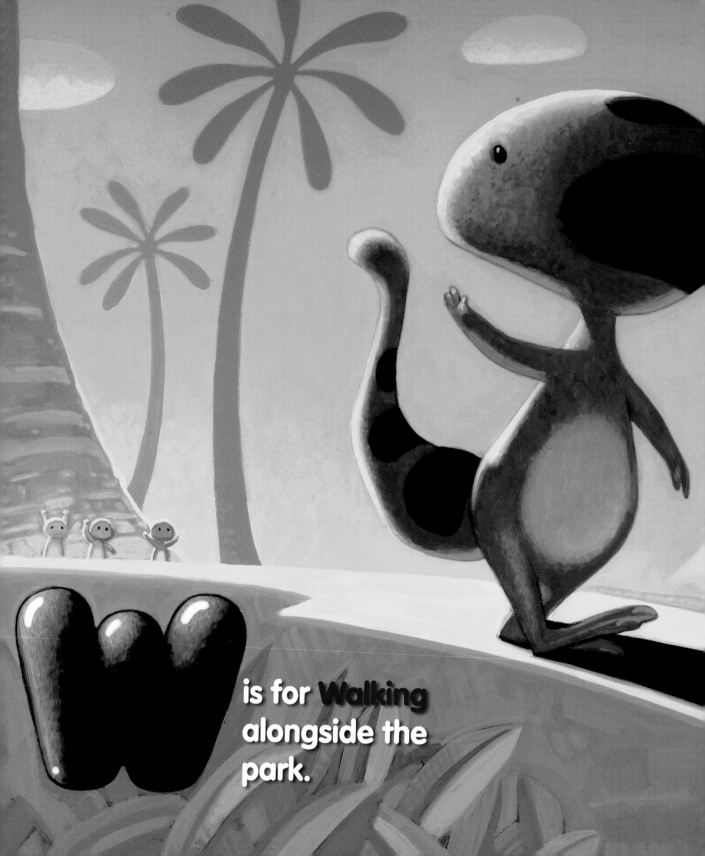

is for **Walking** alongside the park.

is for eXit before it gets dark.

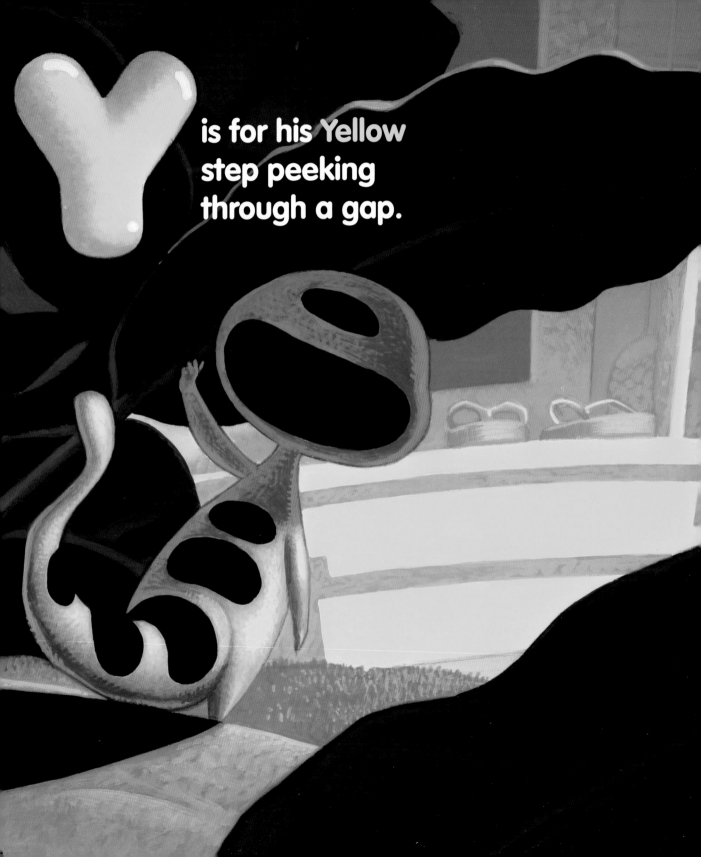

Y is for his Yellow
step peeking
through a gap.

Z is for the **Zori** gecko curls on to nap.